Mr. Rodento
Cleans House
A Story Coloring Book

Written by Sandrina Kurtz

Illustrated by John Kurtz

DOVER PUBLICATIONS, INC.
Mineola, New York

D1510845

When Mr. Rodento, a happy homebody, discovers that he can buy all kinds of things from the catalogs he receives in the mail, he quickly discovers how easy it is to buy *too much*. Grab your crayons or markers, and join the lovable guinea pig as he learns this important life lesson.

Bibliographical Note

Mr. Rodento Cleans House: A Story Coloring Book is a new work, first published by Dover Publications, Inc., in 2015.

International Standard Book Number

ISBN-13: 978-0-486-79391-7
ISBN-10: 0-486-79391-5

Manufactured in the United States by Courier Corporation
79391501   2015
www.doverpublications.com

This is the story of Mr. Rodento, a perfectly happy guinea pig, his tidy house, and what happened to both.

It all started when a catalog showed up in Mr. Rodento's mailbox.
There were many beautiful things to buy in the catalog.

One particular item, a fancy glass bowl, caught Mr. Rodento's eye.
He did not really need the bowl, but it was so pretty. After thinking
about it for awhile, he decided to order it. It was so easy!

Now, all Mr. Rodento had to do was wait for it to be delivered. It suddenly seemed that life without the fancy glass bowl just wasn't complete.

After what felt like an eternity, the happy day arrived. Mr. Rodento watched eagerly as the mail carrier walked up to his door.

Mr. Rodento invited the mail carrier to join him while he opened the package.

The mail carrier thought that Mr. Rodento had made a great purchase! How splendid the little glass bowl looked standing in the middle of his table.

Mr. Rodento could hardly take his eyes of the sparkling new bowl. But he liked his house tidy, so he carried the empty box to the recycling bin. That's when he saw it. There was something else in the box!

It turned out that the company who sold him the fancy glass bowl, tucked a brand new catalog into the box for him to enjoy! Today was his lucky day!

The new catalog was full of the latest kitchen gadgets. It just so happened that Mr. Rodento was fond of his kitchen, and rather proud of his cooking.

Looking through the catalog, he found a nice selection of items he could use. Mr. Rodento thought it would be a shame to pass up the opportunity to own them, and placed his order on the spot.

The next day, right after breakfast, Mr. Rodento found himself flipping through the first catalog again. There were so many nice things to get! He sent for a painting, a rug, a vase, a comfortable chair, and a handy storage hutch.

By now, it may seem that Mr. Rodento had gone a little too far. But in his opinion, the good life had only just begun.

The very next day there was a new catalog in the mail offering the best quality exercise equipment. Mr. Rodento was sure he could use it, so he ordered the largest set!

There were some major changes happening at Mr. Rodento's house. Merchandise arrived, and with it, more and more catalogs. The useful kitchen gadgets showed up, followed by everything else!

These were busy days for Mr. Rodento. Deliveries came from near and far. He spent almost all of his time unwrapping packages and placing more orders for more things! He even found new catalogs on the Internet!

The mail carrier had a hard time keeping up with Mr. Rodento's deliveries. Luckily, special trucks came to deliver the larger items.

They caused quite a commotion! It seemed that the more Mr. Rodento owned, the more he wanted, and the more he thought he needed.

Mr. Rodento's once cozy and orderly house soon became jam-packed with stuff. He had trouble keeping the place clean, and cobwebs started to show up. If he could only find his handy new duster with the long handle!

Luckily, Mr. Rodento also ordered a lawn chair so he could escape from the mounting mess.

But soon enough, Mr. Rodento began to wonder where visitors could sit. Clearly, he needed to order some outside furniture. Then, he thought of a bunch of other things he could use for his yard!

In less than a week, Mr. Rodento's yard looked much the same as his overstuffed house. Besides a set of luxurious outdoor furniture, he also bought a birdhouse and a birdbath. He then decided that a swimming pool was a well-deserved purchase. He also got a great deal on a new set of skis to take on vacation. After all, the pressures of being a homeowner were getting to him!

A barbecue came so Mr. Rodento could cook outside instead of in his cluttered kitchen. He got shiny gardening tools to help make his lawn look nice, shears to cut branches, and umbrellas to create shade.

Because Mr. Rodento found the inside of his house suddenly much smaller than it was before, he hired builders to construct a brand new room. He always liked the open, airy feeling of sunrooms. The builders assured Mr. Rodento that building a sunroom would be "very affordable!"

After just one day of hard work, the builders announced that they were done with Mr. Rodento's new sunroom. It looked straight and strong!

Mr. Rodento was very proud of his sunroom. He felt very relaxed in the new, open space. Now he needed a set of sunroom furniture to truly enjoy the space. He also thought it would be the perfect place for a collection of musical instruments.

Soon, the sunroom was just as packed as the rest of the house.

It had become almost impossible for Mr. Rodento to move around without bumping into something. There wasn't even a place left to cook, inside or out!

Surely, everything he bought was good for *something*,
but Mr. Rodento just didn't feel comfortable anymore.

Even his most beautiful treasures were hidden and covered in dust.

Mr. Rodento began to regret making so many purchases. He wanted his old, simple life back! He stopped placing orders, but that wasn't enough. Something had to be done! Mr. Rodento came up with a great idea. All he had to do was write an advertisement.

Mr. Rodento's ad appeared in the newspaper the very next day.

Neighbors came flocking to Mr. Rodento's house.
Most chose one or two items to buy.

Business went on into the late hours of the evening. The sale was a huge success, and Mr. Rodento felt no regret.

So, what was left for Mr. Rodento? Well, he kept all of his old belongings, as well as his first catalog purchase, the fancy glass bowl. Cleaned off and dusted, it could once again be seen and enjoyed. Mr. Rodento had discovered that *more* can quickly become *too much*!